The BLACK HORSE

by MARIANNA MAYER

pictures by KATIE THAMER

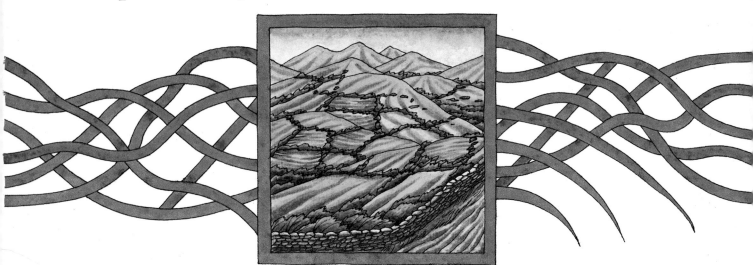

: Dial Books for Young Readers :

E. P. DUTTON, INC.   NEW YORK

The text is dedicated to the fond memory of
Maxmillion — now and always my own *Black Horse*.

M.M.

To my family.

K.T.

Published by Dial Books for Young Readers
A Division of E. P. Dutton, Inc.
2 Park Avenue : New York, New York 10016
Published simultaneously in Canada by Fitzhenry & Whiteside Limited, Toronto
Text copyright ©1984 by Marianna Mayer : Pictures copyright ©1984 by Katie Thamer
All rights reserved
Printed in Verona, Italy, by Arnoldo Mondadori Editore
Typography by Jane Byers Bierhorst
First Edition
W
10 9 8 7 6 5 4 3 2 1

Library of Congress Cataloging in Publication Data

Mayer, Marianna : The black horse.

Summary : A poor Irish prince wins the love of the
Princess of the Mountains after helping her to escape the wicked
Sea King with the magical aid of a mysterious black horse.
[1. Fairy tales. 2. Horses — Fiction.] I. Thamer, Katie, ill. II. Title.
PZ8.M4514Bl   1984   [E]   83-25271
ISBN 0-8037-0075-X   ISBN 0-8037-0076-8 [lib. bdg.]

The art for each picture consists of an ink and watercolor painting,
which is camera-separated and reproduced in full color.

*T*he *Black Horse* is a Celtic folktale with story elements that can be traced to the ancient Celtic race. United by a common language, the nomadic tribes known as the Celts spread westward from Central Europe in the centuries preceding the Christian era. Their power reached its peak in the period between 500 and 100 B.C., and declined thereafter under Roman domination. Many of their tales and legends have lived on in oral tradition, passed down through the centuries, interpreted and adapted by the Gaelic bards of Ireland, Scotland, and Wales. More recently the Celtic Renaissance of the nineteenth and twentieth century sparked a resurgence of interest in Celtic lore. A faint echo of these Celtic myths is present in the fireside tales, such as *The Black Horse*, which we still enjoy today.

The specific source for my version of *The Black Horse* was first written down in the mid-nineteenth century, when it was told in Gaelic by a farmer living on the tiny island of Barra off the coast of Scotland. A noted folklorist of the period, J. F. Campbell, included the story in his manuscript now deposited at the Advocate Library in Edinburgh.

This tale of a young man aided by a magical black steed is filled with symbols that had potent meaning for the Celts. The image of the sea and its Sea King reflects the veneration for water held by a seafaring people, and their belief in the power struggle between the gods of light, the Tuatha Dè Danann, and the gods of darkness, the Fomoiri, who were half-human, half-monster undersea phantoms. Silver and iron, precious metals crafted by these masters of intricate metalwork, were thought to possess supernatural powers to ward off evil spirits. The horse, on which the survival of a nomadic people depended, was worshipped as the symbol of the Celtic horse-goddess. The Druids, holy men of the Celtic religion, claimed the ability to shift their shape and became various sacred animals, in particular the horse. In those pagan times what was worshipped was also sacrificed, and as late as the twelfth century ritual horse sacrifice relating to the rite of enthronement was still practiced in Ulster. Throughout Gaelic lore as well, the image of the horse appears over and over as, for example, in a riddle likening a black horse to the west wind.

Parallels to the tale of *The Black Horse* can be found in literature of other cultures as far east as India. The Ebony Horse, an enchanted flying machine from the *Arabian Nights;* Dapple-grim, the great horse from Norse myth (in at least one version clad in spikes and capable of wondrous feats); and, of course, the winged steed Pegasus from Greek mythology all call to mind the marvelous horse of Celtic legend.

Marianna Mayer

There was once an Irish king who had a son named Tim. Though the kingdom was a very poor one and the King endlessly in debt, he remained till his death a lighthearted, good-natured man. When the King died, his creditors assumed his ramshackle castle and lands, casting his son out into the world with nothing but an old and tired horse.

Without a bitter word Tim shrugged his shoulders and set off. He looked east then west, north then south, trying to decide which way to go to seek his fortune.

"One direction seems as good as another, and yet I suppose..." He paused to think. "Better go with the wind at my back to help me on my way rather than have the wind in my face, telling me to stay."

Tim's prospects seemed slim, even to him. Then one evening, just at dusk, when the sky was streaked with crimson, a great gusty wind blew up from the west. Off in the distance Tim saw among the clouds a tiny speck coming closer and closer. Though by now the west wind had died down, the strange shape continued to speed toward him, growing larger every moment. At last he could see it was a rider on a powerful black horse.

5

"Greetings, sir. Are you not the King's son, Tim?" asked the rider as he dismounted from the magnificent horse.

"Yes, that is who I am. How do you do?" said Tim, astonished.

"Why, not very well, since you are kind enough to ask. I'm ever so weary of riding this difficult horse. He is more than I can handle. Perhaps you would be willing to trade your horse for mine?"

"I'm afraid I would get the better part of that bargain," said Tim with a laugh. "My horse is old, and slow besides."

"That's quite all right with me," the stranger assured Tim. "It would be a nice change to have a quiet horse to ride, and I can promise you that I would treat him well. What do you say?"

Tim didn't need to be asked twice. He knew he was a good rider and he had yearned to ride the splendid animal the moment he saw it.

They made the exchange, and then the stranger was ready to be on his way. "There is something you should know," he said to Tim. "This black horse has great value; there is nowhere in the wide world that he cannot take you. All you must do is ask."

When Tim was alone with the black horse, he climbed on his back, wondering where he should ask to be taken. But not wishing to master such a noble creature, he suddenly said, "I would rather be friends than demand that you do my bidding. Shall we make a pact of friendship instead? On my honor I will ride you well and true, asking only that you take me somewhere you would choose to go."

The black horse snorted his approval and moved his handsome head up and down as if giving his consent. With the speed of a falcon they were off into the sky, and the next thing Tim knew, they were plunging down to the very bottom of the sea. There they came to rest in a marvelous hall where the Sea King was holding court, surrounded by his subjects.

Unfortunately the Sea King was really a wicked sea monster who captured sailors and sometimes swimmers as they drifted through his wide realm. Once in his power, his captives were bound with spells and ever after were forced to remain his unhappy subjects and slaves.

When the Sea King saw Tim and the black horse, he raised his green, slimy webbed hand and waved his magic trident. "Ha, ha!" he exclaimed. "You, rider of the black horse. I lay upon you my spells. Now that you have entered my realm, you cannot resist my commands. The Princess of the Mountains has refused my every offer of marriage, but she will be my bride whether she likes it or not. Bring her to me before the sun rises tomorrow or you shall die."

Once left alone, Tim leaned against the black horse's neck and sighed.

"That is the sigh of a king's son under powerful spells," said the black horse. "But don't worry. Together we will do the task demanded. Come, climb on my back, and we'll be off to the princess's castle in the mountains."

As they began riding, the black horse picked up speed. Faster and faster he flew until they burst from the sea and were high among the clouds again. Soon Tim could see a ring of mountains surrounding a tall peak with a white marble castle built on its very top.

"Now, this is what you must do," said the black horse as they approached the princess's castle. "Once the princess sees us, she will wish to ride me. Tell her you must remain on my back, for I am far too wild for her to ride alone. She is strong-minded, but soon she will agree. I will see to the rest."

It was just as the black horse had predicted. When they arrived, the princess stood among her court guards watching them in awe. The black horse was surely the most remarkable sight anyone had ever seen and the princess begged to be allowed to ride him. Tim was very glad to permit this as long as he was able to accompany her.

"But certainly anyone can ride him," insisted the princess. To prove her point she instructed one of her expert riders to mount the black horse.

As the rider attempted to climb up, the black horse lifted both forelegs and reared in a most frightful manner, throwing the rider to the ground stunned, but unharmed. When the princess saw this, she finally agreed to Tim's terms. As soon as she was settled before Tim upon the horse, they soared high up into the sky, beyond the reach of the crowd and the helpless guards. In a matter of seconds they were in the kingdom of the dreaded Sea King.

The princess looked angrily from Tim to the Sea King. Tim's shame prevented him from meeting her sharp gaze. He felt guilty for what he had done, and he wished with all his heart he could help her, but the binding spells had given him no choice of his own.

The Sea King could barely contain his glee, for at last he thought the princess could not refuse him. "Well done," he shouted. "Now let the wedding take place."

But the princess was a clever girl and, though trickery had entrapped her, she had some tricks of her own that she hoped might help her escape from the wretched King.

First, she thought, she must gain time. Masking her anger, she said, "That, my lord, is not yet possible. It is said that a thousand curses will befall my bridegroom should I be wed without my grandmother's silver cup for good luck. The wedding must wait, I fear, until you can bring it to me."

The Sea King was a superstitious creature, and he shook with fear at the mere thought of such curses. "Rider of the black horse, you are still under spells to do as I command. Bring me the princess's silver cup by sunrise tomorrow so that the wedding may take place."

The princess looked past the Sea King to Tim. Hearing the wicked King's words, she began to understand that Tim was in his power and so was forced to obey. Tim held her gaze for a moment, then nodded in farewell and left the hall.

He went to the black horse, rested his head against the horse's neck, and sighed deeply. "What's this?" said the black horse. "The sighs of a king's son under spells again! Come, my friend. Climb on my back and we'll fetch the silver cup. Don't think I'll foresake you. I know all about the cup, and it will be easy enough for us to get."

As they were flying through the air the black horse said, "The King of the Mountains is mourning the loss of his daughter. Not long ago he lost his son by mysterious means, and now the disappearance of his only other child has made him inconsolable. When we get to the castle, leave me outside and enter as though you are one of the King's company who has come to comfort him. In the course of the evening the silver cup will be passed to all those around the table. See to it that your seat is the last. When the cup is handed to you, take it under your cloak and come out to me. Then we will be off."

Tim followed the black horse's instructions exactly. At dawn the next day they returned to the Sea King with the silver cup.

"You are clever, King's son. But I am more so for having you under my spells," boasted the arrogant Sea King.

Delighted, he began to arrange for the wedding. But the resourceful princess was perhaps more clever than he, for she had yet another condition before the wedding could commence.

In a sweet voice she said, "Oh, but there can be no wedding until I have the silver ring my grandmother and mother wore on their wedding day. It is joined by a two-headed silver serpent that keeps evil from all brides in my family. Without it I simply could not be married."

"Rider of the black horse, I command you," said the Sea King, his face cold with rage. "Bring this silver ring to my bride by sunrise, or you shall die an agonizing death."

The princess could have wept for Tim, for she knew the danger of the task that had been set. This time she caught Tim's gaze and smiled sadly at him as he left. Though Tim felt he must surely be going to his doom, he could not help admiring the clever princess for once more outwitting the Sea King.

Tim went in search of the black horse. When he found him, the black horse was grazing peacefully. Tim sat down beside him and began to sigh heavily.

But before Tim could speak, the black horse said, "Tim, never was there a request made of me that was more difficult than this. Either way we may die. But if we are to be called heroes, there is nothing to be done except for us to try. Here now, climb upon my back. There is a snow mountain, an ice mountain, and a mountain of fire standing between us and the winning of that silver ring. It may cost us our lives to pass them; but I shall do my best and so will you."

"I would never wish you to sacrifice your life for mine," said Tim.

"We are bound together," answered the black horse. "Your fate is linked to mine, and there is no turning back from that now. So come; our time is running short."

Off they went, and as they drew closer to the snow mountain they both felt a deathly cold creep into their flesh. Thickly falling snow blinded their eyes. Yet in one bold leap the black horse landed at the very top of the snow mountain.

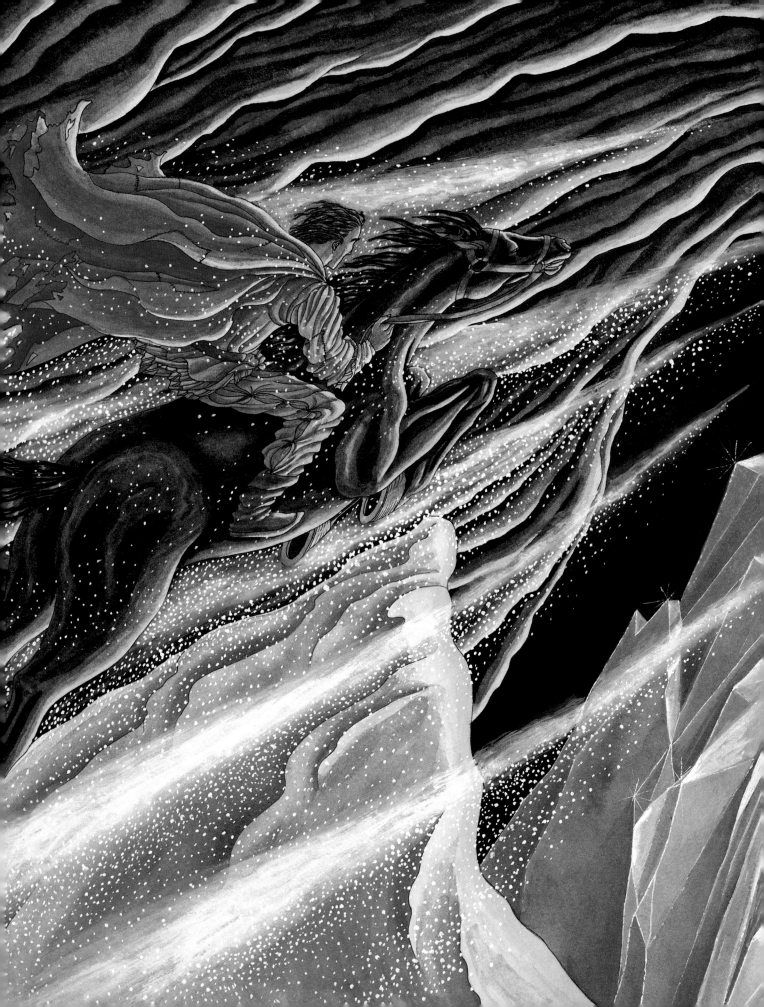

At the next leap they crashed through a wall of glittering ice. Still pushing on toward the slippery ice mountain, their hearts were pierced by ice. Like sharp shards of broken glass, it tore at their flesh. Icicles hung from their hair and limbs; their bodies were nearly frozen. The hooves of the black horse scraped and clashed at the edge of the ice mountain. He struggled to get a footing, then stumbled, and Tim thought they would plunge to certain death. But, no, they reached the top, shattering the crust of ice that covered them. Then the black horse thrust beyond and leapt to the roaring mountain of hungry fire. Biting cold soon became suffocating heat, and Tim clutched the black horse's neck with all his remaining strength. At last, entirely spent, they floated down beside a lake in a green valley beneath the three terrible mountains.

When they had rested, the black horse told Tim, "Go to the blacksmith in the town and have him make me a coat of armor with iron spikes for my every joint."

Tim completed the strange request and returned by nightfall with the armor.

"Now, fasten the armor on me, and make sure that the spikes are secure."

Solemnly Tim arranged the armor around the black horse, but while he was working, a sense of dread filled his heart for his noble friend. When Tim was finished, the black horse stood before him, magnificent in his armor.

"Tim, I must dive into this lake. It will turn to fire and begin to blaze. Now, listen carefully. If you see the fire go out before sunrise, I will return, but if it does not, you must wait for me no longer."

Before Tim could stop him, the black horse plunged into the dark water. Immediately the lake burst into flames. As Tim rushed to follow his friend, the waves of heat from the blaze hurled him backward and nearly knocked him unconscious. He wrung his hands and called after the black horse helplessly, but it was too late. Tim saw no sign of him as the flaming lake raged on and on. Many hours passed while he waited anxiously for the black horse to return.

At dawn Tim watched in amazement as the sun rose from the now dying bloodred flames. Suddenly the lake was calm, and at last the black horse appeared, swimming slowly toward Tim. His armor had vanished, but a single spike with the silver ring upon its pointed end was driven directly into the center of his forehead. Tim gently removed the iron spike from the black horse's head, and to his joy the wound healed instantly without a trace. But the black horse was exhausted. He lay still, hardly breathing as Tim sheltered him with his own body and prayed for him to recover.

As the sun rose still higher the black horse grew stronger and stronger. At last by midmorning he sprang to his feet, tossing his mane proudly. "Do you have the silver ring?" he asked.

"That I do," answered Tim, holding it up in his fist.

"Good. Then climb on my back and let us be off. We have no time left."

But they had to travel as they had come and face the same hard journey through the mountains of fire, ice, and snow. Even so, the mountains were soon behind them, and by the setting sun they returned to the realm of the Sea King.

"You are late," said the Sea King, scowling. "But I will overlook it so long as you have the silver ring."

"I do," said Tim.

"Then there will be no further delays. Let us have it, and the wedding shall begin."

"Our wedding is not as near as you think, King," said the princess. "There is one last requirement. You must build me a castle above the sea, or I will not marry you."

The Sea King became furious. He pounded his fists and roared so loudly that the walls of his hall shook. His subjects fled in every direction, but the princess faced him and said, "You cannot expect me to live beneath the sea forever. I will wither and die. I must have a home of my own on land. Tell me, King, are you not powerful enough to grant me such a simple wish?"

"My bride shall not doubt my power," said the vain Sea King. "Rider of the black horse, do this deed before tomorrow. You shall pay with your life if I am humiliated before my bride." Then he stormed out of the hall, leaving Tim and the princess alone.

"Tim, if you can do this last task, I promise that you will not be made to do another by this fiendish King," the princess told him. "I may have a way to put an end to our misery."

"I will help you in any way I can," said Tim with a bow.

When Tim found the black horse, he sat down upon a rock and said, "There is still one more task I must do, but it's the first I would gladly undertake as the princess herself asked me to. I must somehow build a castle on land, yet as before I have no notion of how I am going to do it without your help."

The black horse began to laugh. "Is that all!" he said. "Well, I always thought the princess was a clever girl; perhaps she is not going to disappoint me now. I have never been asked anything so easy, my lad. Come; climb on my back and let us pick the spot where the castle will stand."

The two friends burst from the sea in a twinkling, and together they chose a lovely grassy knoll. Then the black horse struck the earth seven times with his left foreleg, and suddenly a shimmering castle appeared before the astonished Tim.

At sunrise the princess asked that they go to inspect the interior. The Sea King agreed, but it was very difficult for him to leave the sea. Many of his subjects were forced to help him rise to the surface for he could not have done it alone.

"Now there will be no more delays. We will be married at once," commanded the Sea King.

"Very well," said the princess agreeably. "But we must marry here in the castle."

Then she walked over to the opening of the well where seawater was drawn up for the King. "And does this hole lead us back to the sea?" she asked.

"Yes, it does," answered the King, as he leaned over the ledge of the well to look in.

Suddenly the princess stepped behind him and pushed the Sea King into the well. Down, down, down he fell, back into the sea from which he had come. Then she ordered a stone cover to be placed over the opening of the well, sealing it forever.

The evil king's spells were broken at last. His subjects rejoiced to be free of the horrid ruler, and as they cheered the princess, she went to Tim.

"Rider of the black horse, if I am to be married, it must be to you. You did each task that I asked, and I wish to marry no other man."

"Princess, nothing would make me happier."

The wedding took place that very day. After the ceremony Tim went in search of the black horse.

"This is a good day for you, my friend. You have found someone you can love more than me," said the black horse gently.

"I have not and I won't. I could never love anyone more than you," said Tim.

"I don't mind," said the horse. "It is as it should be, for our work is almost done. I will always be grateful to you. Others have tried to bend me to their will, and when they failed to master me, they tried to force me into obedience. Finding they could not, they soon gave me away. But never before has a rider asked me where I would choose to go. So you see, we have served each other all along. Now you must do something solely for me. Here; raise your sword and strike me a death blow."

"I shall not!" exclaimed Tim, horrified.

"Ha! But you must if you truly love me. It is all I ask; it is all I desire. Do it instantly."

Reluctantly Tim drew his sword, and tears blinded his eyes as he struck the black horse with all his might. Then he cried out in grief and covered his face. The black horse was no more.

"Why do you cry, my brother-in-law?" asked a familiar voice.

When Tim looked up, he saw a fine-looking young man. "Why are you weeping for the black horse?" said the young man. "Don't you realize that you have set him free?"

"I weep because there was never a man or beast I loved more," said Tim.

"Would you take me for him?" asked the young man.

"I would rather the horse."

"But I *am* the black horse, who has been under spells and whom you have helped to become human once more. Together we freed my sister, the princess, and now we will all live in peace," explained the young man.

Upon hearing these words, Tim embraced his friend, and together they returned to the princess. When she saw her brother with her husband, she was overcome with joy.

The feast they arranged was so splendid that there was not a kingdom in the world that did not hear about it. Then the young prince, who had truly been the black horse, returned to his father and took up the ruling of that domain. He lived to a ripe old age, married, and had many fine children. He and Tim always remained friends and those who knew them concluded that never were there two more wise and gentle men.